I TOUCH HOSES

A BENT OAK, TEXAS NOVELLA

BIX BARROW

AUTHOR MISCELLANY

AUTHOR'S NOTE

I Touch Hoses *was formerly a bonus story offered to Bix Barrow newsletter subscribers. The story has not been changed.*

If you find any typos or continuity errors in this book, please email me at bixbarrow@gmail.com. Reporting errors through Amazon does not trigger an alert to the author.

ACKNOWLEDGEMENTS

Thank you to my beta readers, LADK, Beck, and Dani!

Cover by Wicked by Design

Thanks and love to the Sparrows!

RELATED BOOKS

If you're interested in more from the Bent Oak, Texas series, please check out these titles!

Holding On to a Hero (Will, Cole, and Jason's story)

Heart Me Up (Craig and Foster's story)

Head Over Feels (Felix and Malcolm's story)

What's Santa Got to Do with It (Steve and Baz's story)

We Don't Need Another Santa (Phillip and Lucas' story)

Voices Harry (Harry and Mitchell's story) - free if you sign up for my newsletter at BixBarrow.com/Freebies!

BOOK DESCRIPTION

I TOUCH HOSES

What happens when a smoking hot retired rock star finally decides to take a walk on the bi side?

I have no idea. I panicked and tanked our date before I could find out.

When I accidentally overheard Jake Lord, womanizing rock god with a d**k of legendary proportions, say he wanted to come out as bisexual, I never imagined I'd be the first man he'd ask to dinner. What could a famous musician want with me—a guy who's so freaked by what happened on my last job that I'm working as a gardener to try to forget?

I should've turned him down immediately, but he was so adorable—all nervous and awkward—I couldn't stop myself from accepting his invitation.

But after decades of the rock and roll life, Wesley doesn't want to be "Jake Lord" anymore. He's ready to be a dad, a homebody, a guy who rescues kittens. A man like that needs someone who's got their s**t together. And that's definitely not me.

So I bailed before I was in too deep.

Oops. Too late.

I Touch Hoses is part of the Bent Oak, Texas series but is written so it can be read as a standalone. In the series timeline, this story takes place between *Head Over Feels* and *We Don't Need Another Santa*.

CHAPTER 1
WESLEY

Fifty-five years old, fifteen platinum and six multi-platinum albums, fourteen world tours, one child, and untold amounts of sex with more women than I could remember.

And only *now* had I finally grown some balls.

Some being the operative word—the difficult part was yet to come. My stomach was in knots. Not as bad as the first time I'd been on stage, but pretty close.

The Texas Hill Country whizzed by as my son drove us down the highway. Oblivious to my own agitation, he relentlessly laid out his rationale. "You're the only person who calls me Freddy. The law school let me put my preferred name on my diploma, but I want to change it legally before I take the bar. Then I'll start my career with the name I actually use, and people won't laugh when they see my law license."

"But why didn't you change it when you turned eighteen? Or before law school?"

He huffed. The *duh* went unspoken. "Because I didn't want to disappoint you?" Then he gave a sharp laugh. "And my junior year I realized it was a great icebreaker with girls."

"Well, you're single, so it still might come in handy."

Freddy's phone told him to exit the highway. We were almost there. *Don't throw up. Freddy would ask questions.*

"I do just fine without it, old man," he countered. "Don't worry."

"Ouch. Did you have to bring up my age?" The jokes became harder to take every year.

"Speaking of your birthday, I don't understand why you want to spend it with strangers. I hardly get to see you as it is." Freddy would be an excellent lawyer; manipulation was in his blood. It came from his mother's side, of course.

I turned to face him, raising my eyebrows. "I watched you walk across the stage and then spent all weekend with you. Oh, and I'm also moving here. I think you'll live."

Freddy slowed as we approached the ranch's driveway. "Blah, blah, blah. You still feel guilty, though, right?"

This kid. "Don't worry, your skills remain on point."

Freddy stopped in front of the gate. He rolled down his window, examined the speakerbox and camera setup, then pushed the big green button.

"Welcome to Triple Bypass Ranch!" a man chirped. I didn't recognize the voice.

Before Freddy could respond, another voice—definitely Cole's this time—yelled out, "For fuck's sake, Will, it's Triple the Love Ranch and you know it!"

"Um, hi. Jake Lord here." I leaned across Freddy and waved at the camera.

The first voice, apparently Will, was back. "Mr. Lord, can you please exit the vehicle? We only allow approved guests on the property, but we'll send a cart to pick you up."

"My motorcycle's in the bed of the truck." One camera whirred, adjusting its angle. "This is my son, Mac. Can he come in to drop me off?"

Freddy had to add, "Don't worry, I promise to keep the fanboying to a minimum."

Over the speaker we heard Cole again. "Oooh, I like fanboying." Then, "Ouch! What was that for?"

Will again. "Sorry about that. Of course you're welcome to come in. Please follow the driveway past the house to the guest cottage. We'll meet you there."

The gate eased open, and Freddy drove us down a long driveway framed by white wooden fences that fell away as we approached the ranch house. I'm sure it was pretty, but I was completely distracted by something else. Someone else.

Between the driveway and the house, a shirtless and very muscular man rinsed himself off with a garden hose. He was only wearing khaki cargo pants, which had become soaked with water. The man moved the hose in a hypnotic pattern, spilling it first over his shaved head, then his muscled back, then his defined chest. His russet brown skin glistened in the sun, highlighting the lines of his abs and pecs.

What would it be like to run my hands over those muscles and through his dripping beard?

Freddy slowed and, without consciously deciding to, I rolled down my window just as we reached the man.

"Good afternoon," I said inanely, like I was about to invite him for tea. He was even more beautiful up close, with warm eyes and a strong mouth.

"Hey." He eyed me and Freddy with interest, but then he noticed my bike. "Damn, is that a Triumph Bonneville?" Freddy stopped the truck.

"It is." Could I sound more uptight? "It's a 1967 T120R."

The man dropped the hose before stepping forward to get a closer look. He whistled. "Nice."

Freddy poked me in the side, and I snapped my head around. "Ask him if he rides, Dad," he hissed. Right.

I leaned my head out the window. "Do you ride?"

"Yeah, I've got a Yamaha, but it's nothing like this beauty."

Freddy poked me again. "For fuck's sake, Dad. Tell him he can try it out." Good idea.

"Um, you're welcome to take a spin on the Triumph." *Take a spin*? Why was I talking like this? "I'm staying in the guest cottage for a couple of days, so stop by anytime."

The man's face split into a huge smile. "I'd love to." He came over to my window. I couldn't keep my eyes from traveling down his chest to his damp pants, but I jerked my head up as soon as I realized what I was doing. The big smile was still in place. "Hi, I'm Keson," he told me, then glanced at Freddy.

I was mortified. "I'm so sorry. I used to have manners. I'm Wesley. This is my son, Mac." I didn't have to like it, but I respected his wishes regarding what he called himself.

"Nice to meet you. Are the guys waiting for you?"

"Shit, yes. They'll be wondering where we are."

"Just stay on this drive and you can't miss it." He extended his arm to show us the way. Water trailed down his bulging bicep. *Hngh*.

"Nice to meet you!" Freddy caroled.

"You too." Keson waved.

I didn't want to leave, but obligations dictated otherwise. "I meant it about the bike. Come try it out." Freddy took his foot off the brake, and I pushed the button to raise the window back up.

"I withdraw my objections to you staying here on your birthday," Freddy told me.

"*Hmmm?*" The image of Keson with the water hose reverberated in my brain like the last chord of a power ballad in an empty stadium.

"But now I'm dying to know how you got all those women to sleep with you. You have zero game."

"What?"

Before he could respond, we came around a curve, and in front of us was a lovely little house. Cole Washburn waited for us in front with his two partners.

I jumped out as soon as Freddy parked the truck. "Sorry, we stopped to talk to Keson, and he wanted to see the bike."

"Yeah, he's probably dying to ride it." Cole came forward and clasped my hand. "Welcome, Jake. I'm glad you came."

I hadn't been able to avoid the photos online, but seeing the large scar down the side of his famous face was still shocking. But scar or not, Cole gave off a relaxed air he hadn't had when we'd met on the set of a talk show several years ago.

"Thanks so much for allowing me to invite myself over." Cole grinned and turned, no doubt to introduce his partners. "Um," I glanced at all of them. "Now that I'm mostly retired, I've been going by my real name. Please call me Wesley."

Cole's eyebrows arched up, but he nodded. No doubt he

understood the pressure the studio had put on me to have a stage name. *Wesley* didn't scream sex and rock and roll.

Freddy came up beside me. "Hi, there, I'm Mac." We did greetings all round with Cole's partners Jason and Will. Jason grabbed my bag and guitar from the truck while Freddy and Cole helped me unload the Triumph.

"I'm stoked you could bring your bike. I can't wait to go riding tomorrow," Cole enthused. "Keson rides, but we haven't been out together yet. And neither of these guys want to learn."

"Because it's not safe!" Jason shouted from the doorway of the cottage.

Cole and I rolled our eyes at each other. "I'm moving to the area as soon as I find a place to buy," I told him. "Might as well bring the bike now."

Freddy shut the tailgate and came over to hug me. "I'm going to head home." He shook Cole's hand. "Thanks for looking after my dad for a few days." I gasped dramatically, and Cole chuckled.

Freddy flashed me an evil grin before telling Cole, "By the way, today's his birthday."

He ducked away from my attempt to grab him, then jumped in his truck. "Bye, Dad! I'll see you Wednesday!"

———

An hour and change later, I was seated on the back deck of the main house, a glass of iced tea beside me. From here I could see various animals in the fenced areas as well as the big barn and part of the cottage I was staying in.

Cole sank into the Adirondack chair next to mine. He took a sip of his beer and then tackled the subject I'd hoped to postpone until the next day.

"I'm happy to have you visit, don't get me wrong. And I'm glad to have someone to ride my bike with. But we only met that one time. I was pretty surprised when my PA told me you'd reached out."

I sighed and braced my feet on the railing. "Part of the reason is exactly what I told your PA. I'm moving to the area and wanted to get reacquainted."

"And the rest?"

I ran my hands over my face. Time to find those balls I'd grown. I stared at a brown horse in a nearby fenced area. "I'm bisexual."

In my peripheral vision, Cole turned his head.

"Okay."

"But I've never… acted on it," I told the horse.

"So, is this a new realization, or…?"

"Or. I've known since I was a teenager. But back then it was less accepted, and the record label put a clause in my contract."

Cole made a commiserating grunt. "I know what that's like, but I assumed musicians had a little more freedom than Hollywood actors."

I snorted. "Yeah, but I was no David Bowie. I was young and dumb and made a bad deal. By the time I could dictate my own terms, well, I had a reputation." Because I liked women just fine. And I'd dated, fucked, and been seen with lots of them. Sometimes more than one at the same time. My sex life had been fodder for rumors, speculation, and jokes for decades.

This time, Cole's grunt was one of understanding. "You couldn't trust anyone enough to experiment with them."

I nodded at the horse. "Exactly. It was too risky." Then I sighed. "Probably more so in my head than in reality, especially these days."

"For real. And it's not like you would've been declaring yourself not only bisexual but also in a poly relationship or anything."

The blatant irony in his voice made me chuckle, and I finally met his gaze. Cole gave me a rueful grin and finished off his beer.

Here was my opening. "That's why I came to see you."

He frowned. "You want to make a public announcement?"

I shook my head. "No, nothing like that. I need someone safe to… try things out with."

Cole's jaw dropped. "*What?*" He stood up, stiff and thunderous. "Poly doesn't mean we're not exclusive."

Oh, *shit*. "Wait! No! That's not what I meant!"

"Really? It sure sounded like it to me." Cole was loud, and since the back door to the house was propped open, I wasn't surprised when Jason and Will emerged.

"What's going on?" Jason, the former bodyguard, positioned himself between me and Will. Frowning, Will edged around him so he could see better.

Cole snarled, "*Wesley* is bisexual. He came here to 'try things out'." He made air quotes.

I didn't look at Jason and Will. "I chose my words poorly. That isn't what I meant, I promise."

Cole folded his arms and scowled down at me. "Then please enlighten us."

I had royally fucked this up. "I came here for advice. Because you were in the public eye and there was never any gossip about you sleeping with men. I *do* want to try things out, but, like, with men in general. I wasn't meaning *you*, I swear. No offense, but you're not really my type." Cole's mouth fell open. I dared a glance at Jason and Will. They both seemed amused rather than angry. Reassured, I went on. "I came here to ask you how you did it, how you slept with men all those years without anyone talking about it. I'm not afraid to come out, but I don't want anyone selling the story."

Cole, already relaxing, deflated completely. "I get it," he said. "Sorry."

"No, *I'm* sorry." I crossed my arms and rubbed my elbows.

Jason and Will pulled up some chairs, and Jason patted me on the shoulder as he went to sit down. "You'll be a lot sorrier once Cole answers your question."

My stomach dropped. "What do you mean?"

Cole leaned back against the railing and chuckled. "He means you came all this way for nothing. I don't *have* an answer for you. No one gossiped about me sleeping with men because I just *didn't*." He paused. "Well, a couple of times my manager introduced me to other actors who were also in the closet, but that was awkward as hell and not worth the trouble. Mostly I just didn't have sex." Will nudged Cole with his foot. Cole started, then said, "With men, I mean. I just didn't have sex with men."

Well, fuck.

Though I wasn't as disappointed as I would've expected to be. Instead, the tension in my gut eased.

Huh.

Will leaned forward. "So, Wesley, if Cole isn't your type, who is?"

My brain immediately conjured up Keson, broad-shouldered and built. I opened my mouth to answer, but all that came out was, "Umm." My face felt hot.

Will cackled. "You have someone in mind, I can tell. Spill. Who is it?"

Cole rubbed his hands together. "Oooh. I *love* setting people up. Tell us."

It was odd. If we'd been discussing a woman, I'd have told them in a heartbeat. I wouldn't have felt... shy? I might as well have been back in middle school, the way I was blushing. *Fuck me.*

I shook my head. "I don't even know if he likes men."

Cole's entire face lit up with excitement. "We could—"

"Cole, he said no." Will was my favorite. "Wesley has to make this journey on his own timetable."

Cole, former action movie star and multi-millionaire, pouted. "Fine." He carried on mulishly, "If we can't set you up on a date, what about an escort? Or should I say rent boy?" Then Cole slapped his forehead. "Duh! I'm an idiot. Keson!"

What? Was he saying Keson was a rent boy? Escort, rather. Keson was no boy. I blinked in shock as Cole kept talking. "If he's up for it, that is. He's working here as a groundskeeper as a sort of sabbatical so he can decide what he wants to do with his life. He's trying to get over a pretty horrible experience that put him off his old career."

Jason nodded. "He'd be a good option if he's willing. Cole and I met Keson at the first fundraising gala we threw for the ranch. Some jerk tech bigwig had him on contract."

"I hope he likes working here," Will said. "He's really made a difference in the landscaping after only a week." He turned to Jason. "Are we going to offer him a permanent job?"

Jason shrugged. "I want to, but I'll need to talk to Arturo." He looked at me. "He's our ranch manager."

Cole cleared his throat. "Back to the more urgent topic of Wesley's interest in men." He turned to me. "You wouldn't have to sleep with him or anything. And, hell, you might not be Keson't type. But he'd be a great guy to at least go out with. Get used to being in a date-type situation with a man."

"Oh. Um...."

Will saved me again. "Why don't you think about it? We'll feel Keson out in the meantime."

"Okay," I said faintly.

CHAPTER 2
KESON

I HADN'T MEANT TO EAVESDROP.

In my defense, I'd been weeding the flower bed on the side of the house before Cole and Wesley were even on the back deck.

I know. I should have left when they started talking, but I was too curious about Jake Lord. Jake fucking Lord, who sang chart-topping songs and slept with legions of women. Whose real name was apparently *Wesley,* as if he was a plush elephant a five-year-old would drag around. Who'd been adorably awkward telling me about his bike.

And then I heard that same Jake Wesley Lord, known for having a different woman every night, announce he was bisexual. I should have walked away, but I hadn't even considered it.

Because Wesley had never slept with a man. And he wanted to.

I missed a lot of the ensuing conversation because I was staring into space, visualizing Wesley naked on my bed. Imagining his reaction when he touched my cock for the first time. Imagining him split open on my dick—

Whoa. Wesley was nothing like the guys I'd been attracted to in the past. I couldn't deny he was a snack, even if he probably had twenty years on me. His eyes were a pale brown, nearly gold color that I could drown in. His hair was almost white on the closely-shaved sides and then still mostly black on top, which was cut longer to flop over his forehead. I hadn't stood next to him yet, but I thought he was taller than my five foot ten. His height combined with his thin frame would have my mother using the term *beanpole.*

"*Pssst!*"

I started, spinning to see Tracey, Cole's PA, standing next to the front of the house. She gestured furiously at me to come toward her.

I threw one longing look toward the back deck before I abandoned my tools and reluctantly went to see what she wanted. Tracey didn't speak. She just grabbed my wrist in an implacable grip and dragged me into the house to the kitchen. She pointed at the sink and said, "Wash your hands."

"Um, why? I still need to put my tools away."

Tracey glared. "So you have a plausible alibi that you weren't standing in the flower bed eavesdropping on Cole's conversation with Jake Lord."

She was mean, but she had a good point. I started scrubbing. Tracey took a glass out of the cabinet and filled it with ice.

"Now," Tracey demanded, "I heard everything up until Jason and Will went outside and shut the door. Why haven't they kicked Jake Lord's skinny ass off the ranch yet?" She put the glass under the refrigerator's water dispenser.

"No need. Stand down. You missed the explanation; he didn't mean it the way it sounded. He wanted advice, not sex." Or at least not sex with Cole.

Tracey eyed me dubiously. "Uh huh. Advice on what exactly?"

I really hated to gossip, but Wesley didn't need a pissed-off Tracey hunting him down. I didn't know her well, but she'd been Cole's personal assistant for ages. She wouldn't pass anything on.

"He wanted to know how Cole kept his bisexuality hidden for all those years while still sleeping with men."

Tracey stared at me a moment, then burst out laughing. "Holy shit, I bet he was disappointed." She stopped laughing and put a hand to her mouth. "He wants to sleep with guys, but keep it on the DL?"

"Yeah, I kind of tuned them out after that." Because I was fantasizing about Wesley.

Before Tracey could respond, the back door opened, and everyone came inside. I quickly took the glass from Tracey and gulped the water down. *Nothing to see here, just a guy who's been hanging out, drinking his water for way too long to overhear anything.*

I put the glass in the dishwasher. Tracey walked over to introduce herself to Wesley and I gave everyone a casual wave on my way out of the kitchen to the front door. Only Jason narrowed his eyes at me; he knew where I'd been working earlier. But he said nothing, so I made my escape.

———

I didn't finish for the day until almost 8pm. It wasn't like I had a deadline to weed the flowerbeds or spread the mulch, but anything was better than being at home. My roommate Del was working tonight, so going back to the apartment meant being alone with my stupid thoughts, full of if-onlys and hindsight. Spreading mulch was more than preferable.

As if she was psychic, the primary reminder of my stress and regret chose that moment to text me.

POPPY

Me, wishing you'd come visit

[photo]

Her fake pout made me smile before memories of that day took over. I stuffed my phone in my pocket and finished putting my tools away in the equipment shed that backed up to the horse barn. I'd never seen a shed so spotless, and I was always extra careful not to track dirt or grass inside. Arturo, the ranch manager, was my boss while I was working here. He mostly left me alone, which was a complete gift to me right now, and I didn't want to give him a reason to complain.

The barn itself boasted a full bathroom, including a shower stall. I loved not having to ride home in my sweaty clothes. Showering usually helped me shut off my brain, but tonight thoughts of Wesley warred with my typical obsessive rehashing of my worst mistake.

I forced myself to think instead about the plants along the side of the main house where I'd been weeding today. Other than learning a certain rock star's sexuality swung in my direction, I hadn't been pleased.

Jason's mom, bless her heart, had picked out the shrubs and perennials when she'd visited several months ago. She was from California, not Texas, and her choices wouldn't last the summer. I shuddered thinking about the amount of water that would be wasted trying to save the plants.

I'd be gone by then, I thought wistfully, but I could give

Arturo a list of what to plant instead. My parents had owned a nursery, so I'd been raised around green growing things.

I dried off and got dressed. I didn't want to lose my ideas, so I stuffed my dirty clothes into my backpack and headed to Arturo's office in search of paper and a pen. I patted horse noses along the way to the other end of the barn.

Arturo's office door was open a crack, and the desk lamp was on. That was weird. Arturo ran a pretty tight ship. I couldn't imagine him forgetting to turn out a light.

Nothing looked out of place, so I shrugged it off. I didn't figure Arturo would appreciate me touching anything on his desk, but there was a credenza behind it that hosted a printer at one end. Bingo. I removed a few pages of paper from the tray, then I snagged the cheapest-looking pen from the cup on the desk.

Standing at the credenza, I quickly sketched a rough outline of the side of the main house on one page, and the front on another. Might as well do this right.

I drew rough placeholders for new shrubs and perennials, and along the side I made a list of different native plants to be mixed and matched depending on what color flowers they might want. The third sheet of paper went on top. I wrote Arturo's name and added, "To be opened upon the inevitable death of the hibiscuses".

When I turned to leave, my eyes fell on an open cardboard box on the floor, mostly tucked under the desk. To one side of the box was a pan of kitty litter, and to the other side were bowls of water and kibble.

The office door had been open. *Shit.*

I made a quick circuit of the room, looking underneath the

desk and behind the credenza. Nothing. *Shit, shit*. I went next door to the tack room. No cat.

I searched every stall as fast as I could without spooking the horses. No cat.

Desperate, I checked the shed, even though I'd shut the door behind me. Nothing.

The immediate area around the barn was well-lit with pole lights, but beyond the lights the darkness was almost impenetrable, even with my phone's flashlight. That fucking cat could be anywhere.

Time to call for reinforcements.

> Arturo's office door was open. It looks like he's keeping a cat in there? I couldn't find it anywhere in the barn or shed. Help!

JASON

> Fuck. It's a kitten. A black kitten we'll probably never find in the dark. Give us a minute to get dressed and we'll come down there with flashlights

> Thx I'll keep looking

I peered into the dark. A black kitten. *Fuck*. I hadn't heard any coyotes, but it wouldn't surprise me to find some on the ranch. And besides coyotes there were still owls, snakes, foxes, and who knows what else out there in the night.

Shit.

CHAPTER 3
WESLEY

I was still puzzling about why I hadn't been more disappointed that Cole didn't have a solution to my *how-to-discreetly-sleep-with-a-man-for-the-first-time* dilemma. My initial reaction—my *current* reaction—was relief. But why?

That question bounced around in my head from the moment Cole told me his story, all the way through dinner, and even during the last-minute birthday Oreos and ice cream.

Cole, Will, and Jason had been friendly and entertaining, and I hoped I'd kept up my end of the conversation. Finally, desperate for some time alone, I'd pleaded weariness and retreated to the guest cottage.

After stripping down to my t-shirt and boxers, I went to the kitchen and opened all the cabinets to see what snacks I could find. Stress eating? You betcha.

Plates, check. Glasses, check. Serving dishes, check. One of the larger cabinets was dedicated to liquor. I came face-to-face with a bottle of Macallan single malt and felt victorious when I wasn't even tempted.

The next cabinet held the motherlode. Oreos again, but also several other varieties of cookies, along with chips, crackers, and almost any other sweet or salty munchie you could want.

Laden with a glass of ice water and a giant combo box of Hostess Cupcakes and Twinkies, I made my way to the sofa and settled in. An enormous TV took up most of one wall, but I was more interested in brooding, so I put my back against the armrest and stretched my legs out along the cushions.

Okay, time to figure this out. Why was I relieved? Was it because I didn't really want to sleep with a man? I snorted and shoved a Twinkie into my mouth. I'd wanted to sleep with a man my entire adult life. My reaction to Keson this afternoon just reinforced it.

Was I not ready? I shook my head. I'd been ready for a while now.

Was it the risk of discovery? I'd be media fodder for weeks once I was spotted dating a man. That didn't bother me, but Freddy needed to know first.

I wasn't really sure why I hadn't already told him I was bisexual. Every time I started to, I hesitated, which was idiotic. Freddy's best friend, his future partner in their law firm, was openly gay. Why was it so hard for me to come out to my son? I'd tell him, I promised myself. Once I found a man to date, Freddy would be the first to know. Well, hopefully the first after this hypothetical man. Whatever.

I washed down the Twinkie with some water and pictured myself in public with a man. Walking down the street, holding hands. Sitting on the grass at an open-air concert. Grabbing takeout on the way home. Laughing and cuddling on the sofa. Kissing our way into the bedroom after the movie was over.

My hand, about to pull the next snack cake from the box, stilled.

I was picturing a relationship, not a hookup.

Me, the perpetual slut, famous not only for my music but also for how many women I'd slept with. Who'd never had a relationship that'd even lasted a year.

I'd tried the exclusivity thing, but no one ever held my interest. I'd gotten bored and wanted to move on. Freddy's mother and I had broken up when she was five months pregnant. We'd been great co-parents, but we hadn't had enough spark to stay together romantically.

But now, apparently, I was ready to settle down. I don't know why I hadn't realized it til now. I'd been taking steps for the past two years, retiring from making albums and touring. Planning to buy a house here so I could be near Freddy.

Fuck me, I was having a mid-life crisis.

Which is why I'd been relieved Cole couldn't help me find a discreet hookup. I didn't want a transaction, a quick and meaningless fuck.

I wanted a boyfriend.

I gobbled down a Hostess Cupcake, tossing the plastic wrap on the coffee table.

Okay, so now my goal was to find a boyfriend. How did people find boyfriends?

Well, you idiot, how did you find the girlfriends you've had?

Ugh. The few girlfriends who'd lasted more than a weekend, I'd met at parties or backstage. That idea was a non-starter. I wasn't touring anymore, I was no longer interested in endless partying, and I didn't want to date someone who was.

What did that leave me with? Blind dates? Friend set-ups?

I grimaced and pulled out another Twinkie. My mind wandered back to Keson, how his muscles had gleamed with water in the sunshine. How his warm brown eyes had lit up at the sight of my bike, not at the sight of a celebrity. I wished I'd had time to examine how his wet pants had clung to his body.

Would Keson go out with me if I asked? I didn't care about his past as a sex worker, though I couldn't deny feeling pleased for him that he was exploring other career options. He was probably in his late twenties, so he had plenty of time to figure out what he wanted to do, especially with supporters like Cole, Jason, and Will.

Maybe tomorrow, after Cole and I returned from our ride, I'd find Keson and remind him of my offer for him to ride my bike. Then I'd have an opportunity to ask him out.

Even if he turned me down flat, asking Keson out would give me some practice. I scrunched up my face. My nerves needed to settle the hell down. I was a fucking rock star. I could ask anyone out, man or woman, without turning into an awkward teenager.

And if Keson agreed to a date, I'd call Freddy and tell him I was bisexual.

That decided, I picked up my phone to distract myself with another round of looking at houses for sale. Austin real estate, residential and commercial, was insane. It wasn't only me. Freddy and Tobias were having huge problems finding office space for their future law firm.

Maybe tomorrow when Cole and I were out on our bikes I could get a feel for the Bent Oak area. Out here I'd be able to have a bit of land or at least a decent-sized yard. I wouldn't mind having a dog, or any pet really.

Just as I was picturing Keson walking a dog with me, I heard a tiny *meow* from outside the front window. I froze. Had I imagined the sound because I'd been thinking about pets? No, it came again.

I tossed my phone aside and ran to the front door.

No cat. I trotted down the walkway until I was outside the circle of the porch light, then I turned to look at the cottage. The cat still wasn't visible from this angle.

"Kitty?" I called, feeling all kinds of foolish.

And yet it meowed right back. I called again, then followed the meows to the flowerbed next to the porch. Why hadn't I brought my phone outside so I'd have a flashlight?

Eventually I found it, a tiny black kitten who purred when I picked it up and held it against my chest.

"How did you get here? Are there more of you? Where's your mother?" I needed to call Cole.

But first I took the kitten into the house. It blinked at me under the lights and purred louder. Its eyes were blue-green and it had long fur, ending in tufts on the tips of its ears. It was black all over except for one white whisker. My heart squeezed. Well, shit, maybe I'd be getting a pet sooner rather than later.

"Are you hungry, little guy? Or girl?" I turned the kitten over, but I couldn't see any obvious sex organs. Did that mean it was a girl? Maybe Cole would know.

I clasped the kitten to my chest with one hand and opened the snack cabinet with the other. I quietly whooped in triumph when I found a can of tuna. "These guys get five stars for stocking this place," I told the kitten. Luckily the can had a pull-tab, but I didn't doubt a can opener lurked somewhere nearby.

Soon the kitten was on the floor, eating and purring. I filled a bowl with water and set it down as well. "Okay, kitty. I'll be right back." I jogged to the living room and grabbed my phone.

Cole answered on the first ring. "Hey, Wesley. Is everything okay?"

"Yeah, sorry to bother you, but I found this kitten—"

"*Kitten*! You found the kitten! Is it alright?"

"Yeah, I think so. I gave it some tuna and it's eating."

"Oh, my god, thank you. Keson told us it was missing—oh, shit, I need to call off the search." He hung up.

I looked at the kitten, who was sitting next to the now half-empty bowl of tuna, licking its paw and rubbing its face. "Damn, you're too cute."

I picked it up and took it into the living room. When I sat on the couch, it immediately began kneading my belly, purring loudly. Cole called back a few minutes later.

"Okay, Keson's going to come get the kitten."

"Really? I mean, he's welcome to stay here with me."

Cole's voice turned coy. "Keson or the kitten?"

I groaned. "You know I meant the kitten." Cole chortled in my ear.

"Sure. But Keson's probably almost there. He's been working since dawn or something, then he had to search for the kitten, so can you ask him if he wants a drink or a snack before you kick him out?" Cole *sounded* sincere, but I got the feeling he had another agenda.

"Cole, are—" A firm knock echoed through the cottage.

"Oh, sounds like he's there. Have a good night. Bye!" And he was gone.

Shaking my head, I lifted the kitten again and walked to the door. Keson waved at me through the window. I was sorry to note he was fully dressed.

When I opened the door, I said, "Hey, Keson. Good to see you again." That sounded normal, right?

The kitten decided it didn't want to be held anymore and climbed up my chest to my shoulder, where it hung on with its claws. "Ouch." I winced but managed not to shake the kitten off.

Keson looked me up and down and a broad grin took over his face. Fuck, I'd forgotten I was only wearing a t-shirt and boxers. My skinny, pasty-white arms and legs were on full display.

"The kitten seems to like you."

I felt self-conscious, though I didn't know why. "Yeah. I mean, I told Cole he could stay here."

Keson smirked. "I see how it is. Hey, you want me to go back to the barn and get his litterbox and food?" Mentioning food must have been a trigger, because Keson's stomach let out a loud growl.

I laughed. "I've got food for him here, and I'm sure I can figure out a litterbox. Why don't you come in and help yourself to something to eat? There's a bunch of sandwich stuff in the fridge." I stepped back and gestured him inside.

"If you're sure?" He gestured at my lack of clothing. "Looks like you were getting ready for bed."

"Nah, just hanging out on the couch." Oh, *shit*. I'd never be able to hide the Twinkies and Hostess Cupcakes in time. Or the wrappers.

Keson moved past me into the living room. "Oooh, Twinkies!" He looked at me hopefully.

"Help yourself." I shut the door. Keson took one Twinkie out of the box, then headed for the kitchen, tearing at the wrapper as he walked.

"Man, I love these things." He stuck one end of it in his mouth and then opened the fridge.

"Take whatever you want. I don't know who stocked this place, but it's got almost everything you could ask for." Keson made appreciative noises and started pulling lunch meat and condiments out of the fridge.

I set the kitten down on the floor next to the tuna again, but it seemed more interested in watching Keson.

"Does this guy have a name?" I asked Keson.

"No. And I'm not actually sure it's a boy. Cole told me he was left in a box at the front gate this morning."

"And they were keeping him in the barn?"

"Yeah, Arturo had him in his office. One of the ranch hands probably didn't know the kitten was in there and didn't shut the door."

I poured Keson a glass of water, and he leaned against the counter to eat his sandwich. I poked around in the cabinets until I came up with a decent-sized but shallow plastic container that I didn't think anyone would mind my sacrificing for a litterbox. Then I tore up a bunch of paper towels into tiny pieces. The kitten sniffed the container but didn't get in, so I picked him up and set him inside. After one tentative swipe with a paw, the kitten spun around in circles before plowing back and forth with its front paws outstretched, creating a wake of paper towel pieces.

Keson looked at the kitten and the makeshift litterbox doubtfully.

"I guess we'll just hope for the best," I said, shrugging. "Let's go sit down. I'm sure you're exhausted."

"Yeah, I'm not looking forward to the ride home." Keson popped the rest of his sandwich into his mouth and carried his water glass into the living room.

I picked up my phone. It was after 9:00pm. Keson settled into one end of the couch and leaned his head back on the cushion with a groan.

"Why don't you just stay here tonight?" His head came back up. "There's a second bedroom. It isn't safe to ride when you're so tired."

Keson pushed himself upright, then looked at me with a hesitant expression. "I'd appreciate that, but I need to tell you a couple things first." My eyebrows shot up. "I was working in the flowerbeds on the side of the main house this afternoon when you and Cole were out on the back deck."

Icy cold rushed through my body. He'd heard us? Oh, god. Cole had talked about Keson's former occupation.

Keson held up his hands. "I'm so sorry. I didn't mean to eavesdrop, but I heard you tell Cole you're bisexual."

"Oh. Um, yeah." I didn't know where to look.

"Congrats on coming out, man. Even if it was just to the guys." He made a face. "And me. Sorry. I'm under NDA if it helps."

That made sense; he was working around Cole, who needed

to protect his privacy. "Oh, um, I'm not upset you know I'm bisexual. Did you, um, hear the rest of the conversation?"

He grinned. "Your voices were pretty loud during the part where Cole accused you of wanting to sleep with him and you had to tell him he wasn't your type."

I put my hands over my face. "That was so embarrassing."

He threw his head back and belly-laughed. "You'll think it's funny a few years from now."

"Maybe."

"But that was all I heard before I went inside," he said. I sagged into the couch in relief until Keson cleared his throat. "The other thing is, I'm probably here under false pretenses."

I blinked. "Probably?"

"Yeah, Cole did officially send me to pick up the kitten." Okay?

"But," he said wryly, "He dropped a lot of innuendos, so I'm pretty sure he was also hoping I'd pop your gay cherry."

After a second of shocked silence, I couldn't help but bark out a laugh at his phrasing. I felt uncomfortable with Cole trying to pressure Keson to solve my sexual deficits though. It didn't sound like he'd *paid* Keson to be here, but still.

"Uh, I don't think—"

Keson raised his hands again. "Hey, your decision completely."

I cocked my head at him. "Are you saying you'd *want* to have sex with me?" My dick was getting very interested in this conversation.

"Fuck, yes." He gestured at me. "You're smoking. I'm more than down for it."

My face was burning hot. Me, the man-whore of rock and roll, blushing when someone said they wanted to sleep with me. *Fuck.*

"Um," I looked at my hands, then forced myself to meet Keson's eyes. "It's not that I'm not flattered. And interested."

Keson slapped his hands to his cheeks, giving me a faux-shocked face. "Are you giving me the *it's-not-you-it's-me* speech? Bruh, you can turn me down. I'm a big boy; I can take it."

I raised my hands. "What I was *trying* to say is that I'm not in the market for a quick fuck. I've been there, done that."

"Quite a few times, if the tabloids are to be believed." He smirked. I picked up the box of snack cakes and pitched it at his head. He caught it easily, dammit.

"If you'll let me finish?"

"I'm not stopping you." He winked. Fucker.

"I'm getting older." I paused but he just raised his eyebrows. "I want sex to mean something. Something that could lead somewhere."

Keson nodded. "I get that."

"So, the thing is, I wanted to ask you out."

His face went slack. "What?"

Shit. Was he going to say no? *Gah!* Asking someone for a date hadn't been this nerve-wracking since high school.

I pressed on. "I said, I want to ask you out. Um, to dinner. Not for tonight, obviously. I'll be here til Wednesday, so maybe tomorrow? If that doesn't work for you, I'm staying in downtown Austin. So I can meet you somewhere. Or... whatever." I trailed off and pressed a hand over my eyes. "Shoot me now."

When I found the courage to peek between my fingers, Keson was looking at me quizzically.

"What's the matter?" I asked him. "You don't have to say yes. Really, it's fine."

He shook his head. "It's not that. It's just, why me? You're a rock legend. You could have anyone." He tapped his chest. "I'm a nobody. I'm... in between careers and right now I'm pulling weeds and digging holes all day. Sex, I get. People want me for sex. But you're talking about *dating*."

Fuck, Keson should be the last person to feel insecure. "I am. I'm talking about dating, about the possibility of a relationship. I don't care what your career was before or what it is now, as long as you're doing something you enjoy. You're hot as fuck. When I saw you spraying that hose all over yourself earlier, I almost swallowed my tongue." That earned me a cocky grin. "Cole, Jason, and Will had only good things to say about you, and just based on this conversation, I think you'd be fun to go out with. That's about all anyone ever has before a first date. So what do you say? Will you go to dinner with me tomorrow?"

Keson hesitated, but then produced a shy smile. "Why not? Let's do it."

"Really?" I squeaked. No one would believe I'd done voice and breathing exercises almost every day since I was eighteen.

"Really." He had a lovely laugh, even if it was at my expense. Not that I could blame him. Good thing Freddy wasn't here.

"Freddy!" I shouted, startling Keson. "I have to tell Freddy!" I twisted around looking for my phone. I'd just had it.

"Um, who's Freddy?"

Shit. "Mac. Mac is Freddy. He hates his name." Finding the phone right where I'd set it down earlier, I dialed.

Keson's eyebrows lifted as the phone rang.

"Oh, right," I said as it went to voicemail. "He's out with his friends. I'll just call him tomorrow."

"Um, okay?"

I was an idiot. "Sorry. I promised myself I'd tell Freddy I was bisexual before I went on a date with a guy."

"You haven't told him yet?"

"No. I just haven't had the balls, I guess."

"Damn, that's too bad about your balls." The cocky grin was back.

I wrinkled my nose. "Do I want to ask?"

"Because I was hoping you'd put out on the first date. But if you don't have any balls...." He shrugged and poked around in the box for another Twinkie.

I yanked the couch cushion from behind me and hurled it at him, knocking the box to the floor. The remaining pastries spilled out across the rug.

Keson gasped. "You monster! Look what you've done!" He dove for the snack cakes, but I got there first, grabbing up the ones I could reach. "No! You don't deserve them!" he shouted.

Laughing, we ended up on the floor in an odd game of Hungry Hungry Hippos, snack cake-style. Once we'd collected all we could hold, we faced each other on our knees, panting and grinning. I had six rather squished snack cakes tucked between my forearms and my belly. Keson held another five, though his were in slightly better shape. The rest were mostly under the coffee table.

He was beautiful. He exuded happiness and fun, and I'd never wanted anyone so much. I dropped my spoils on the floor and knee-walked over to him. "I don't want to have sex before our first date."

Keson stared at my mouth. "I understand."

I pulled the pastries out of his hands and threw them over my shoulder in the general direction of the coffee table. "But that doesn't mean we can't make out."

"Shit, yeah," he breathed and leaned in, tilting his head slightly.

Lips and tongue, those were familiar. But Keson's beard felt new and exciting against my mouth and face. His chest was flat, broad and firm. When his arms came up around my back and the muscles in his pecs flexed, my hips involuntarily humped into his.

Keson grabbed my ass and pulled our groins together. *Fuuuuuck.* My boxers were so thin I could feel the heat of him through his jeans. I gasped against Keson's mouth, and his lips turned up. "If you like this, just wait til tomorrow night when we're naked."

"Jesus." I was in danger of passing out merely from the mental image.

I startled when Freddy's ringtone filled the air.

Reluctantly I disengaged from Keson and crawled over to the couch where I'd left my phone. At my age you couldn't just hop up from being on your knees.

"Hey, Dad," Freddy greeted me. "Sorry I missed your call. What's up?"

"Hey, um. I didn't mean to interrupt...." I trailed off as Keson jumped to his feet. Fucking young knees. With one hand he stretched out the hem of his t-shirt to create a pouch, and with the other he gathered the Twinkies and Hostess Cupcakes and dumped them inside.

"Are you working out? You're breathing pretty hard."

"What? No. I'm fine. I'm, um, about to go to bed." Keson raised his eyebrows and kept picking up pastries.

"What did you need?"

After leveraging myself to my feet, I stalked Keson as he speed-walked toward the kitchen.

"Dad?" Oops.

"Right, sorry. I just wanted to tell you I'm bisexual." Fuck, I'd said it. Keson pumped one fist while he kept walking. My face flushed.

Freddy whooped. "Fucking fina—I mean, thanks for telling me, Dad. You know I love you and I don't care who you date or what gender they are as long as you like them."

With his free hand Keson opened the fridge and pulled out a beer. He waved it in my direction inquiringly, and I shook my head no. From this angle I could see he was holding his shirt high enough that his abs were visible. My fingers itched to explore them. Or maybe I should use my tongue.

"Dad?"

"Huh? Oh, sorry, Freddy. I've, um, I've got to go."

"Wait. Is someone—never mind. Ew, I don't want to know. See you Wednesday." I set the phone on the counter absently, then drifted toward Keson.

"That seemed to go well," he remarked

I reached out and caressed his abs. *Damn.* His muscles were firm, his skin soft. The barest hint of hair crinkled beneath my fingers as I ran them below his navel.

"Fuck, Wesley." The beer bottle clinked as it hit the counter-top. I put my hand on the back of Keson's head and pulled him in to meet my kiss. As our lips touched, I let go and grabbed him around his ribcage. I pulled us together as hard as I could, smashing his hoard of snack cakes flat.

Keson howled and shoved me away. I skipped back out of his reach, and the pastries fell to the floor.

"My precious!" Keson shouted. Despite the damaged snack cakes, our shirts were unexpectedly pristine.

While Keson recovered his treasures, I backed out of reach. The kitten was on the counter next to the sink, so I lifted it up like a furry shield.

Keson's chuckles filled the kitchen. He held up a Twinkie. "They're fine," he said.

I lowered the kitten to the counter. "What?"

He examined each Twinkie and Cupcake in turn. "No, wait. This one's packaging burst." He tossed a Cupcake to me. Other than the torn plastic wrap, the only damage was a crack through the icing. The pastry itself seemed unharmed.

Keson poked at the Twinkies. "They've all gone back to their original shape."

I stepped closer so I could prod at them as well. "Damn. That's kind of creepy."

Keson took back the Cupcake with the torn packaging and unwrapped it. "You're lucky they're still edible. But my revenge would've been fun."

I scoffed. "I can take anything you can dish out."

"You sure? I'm really good at edging." He winked. "Really, really good."

I stared at him, my mouth hanging open. Keson swiped his forefinger through the Cupcake's cream filling, then painted it over my lips before shoving his finger into my mouth. I wrapped my tongue around it. The cream filling was sweet, his finger warm and calloused. My dick hardened instantly.

"Fuck." Keson's eyes were intent on my mouth and his nostrils flared as his breath came faster. "How soon does our first date start?" he asked.

Not fucking soon enough.

CHAPTER 4
KESON

I GROANED WHEN MY ALARM WENT OFF. I'D STAYED UP WAY TOO late, and now I had to run home for some clothes. Good thing Wesley and I hadn't shared a bed last night. I'd have an even harder time getting up.

I splashed water on my face and put on the t-shirt Wesley had handed me last night. The fit was a little tight, but I wasn't going to complain about getting my very own vintage Jake Lord concert t-shirt. Okay, it wasn't really mine, but it would be as soon as I got home and hid it in the back of my closet.

I just needed to make it off the ranch before I ran into Cole. If he saw me wearing Wesley's t-shirt, the interrogation would be relentless.

I quietly opened the bedroom door. Wesley's door was open a crack, probably in hopes that the kitten would sleep with him. That furball was *so* getting adopted.

Before going to bed, I'd jogged down to the barn to get my backpack and write a quick note to Arturo about where the kitten was. I'd also brought the litterbox back with me. I didn't trust the kitten to use Wesley's paper towel and Tupperware creation.

I detoured to the kitchen to put my glass in the sink and leave a note with my phone number for Wesley.

I halted when I saw the disaster. The litterbox had been overturned and used kitty litter was spread out over several feet. The roll of paper towels had been unfurled completely, then shredded. The water bowl had ended up about six feet from where we'd left it, empty. Fortunately a mound of paper towel shreds had soaked up the water.

Fuck. How the hell had I slept through all this?

"Hey." Wesley's voice behind me was tentative.

I turned. He was still wearing his boxers and t-shirt, and that fucking kitten was riding his shoulder like the boss it was.

"Hey, good morning." I realized I was still holding my water glass, so I sidled into the kitchen to put it on the counter. "Look at what your little friend was up to all night."

"Oh. My. God." Wesley put his hand on his forehead. The kitten surveyed his handiwork with smug satisfaction.

"I'll get a trash bag." I opened the cabinet under the sink and found a box of them. Wesley sat the kitten down on the counter—good thing my mom wasn't here—and helped me clean everything up.

Just as I tossed the trash into the bin outside, Arturo drove up. He was probably Wesley's age, but years of working in the sun—and, let's face it, not being rich as fuck—made Arturo appear at least a decade older. He stopped and rolled down his window, so I told him I needed to run home and change before coming back to work.

"Keson, it's not like I'm actually your boss. You don't need to worry about some sort of schedule."

I shrugged. The whole situation of working here while not really working here was awkward as hell. "Oh, hey, I left you a note. The kitten that was in your office, I think Wesley's kind of taken him in." I jerked my head back toward the guest cottage. Arturo nodded, blank-faced, but he eyeballed my t-shirt.

Trying to distract him, I rambled on. "I finished the supply order yesterday, and I also left you some notes about the shrubs around the main house. What's there now won't survive the summer."

Arturo seemed pleased. "Thanks. I noticed the other day those plants weren't looking too healthy. I've been meaning to ask you about them."

"I made you a list of a bunch of native plants that'll be pretty but also survive. I also want to add in some bee-attracting plants all around the ranch, though, so give me a couple of days on that."

"Thanks, Keson. Hey, this afternoon can you help me set up the new chicken coop?"

"Sure, no problem." Arturo waved and resumed his drive to the barn.

Back inside, Wesley had started the coffee, and he was almost finished making breakfast. Bread was in the toaster, bacon was in the pan, and he was whisking eggs in a bowl. "Wow, you didn't have to do all this," I told him.

He turned a little pink. It was adorable. "It's not any trouble. You can't work all day on an empty stomach."

I couldn't help myself. I walked over and kissed him on the cheek. "Thank you. I appreciate it."

Wesley smiled and turned even redder. He didn't say anything, just nodded.

The little hell-cat was nowhere to be seen as I kissed Wesley goodbye on my way out the door. The sun was almost completely up as I strolled down to get my bike.

I shouldn't have been surprised to see Cole and Jason leaning against the barn, casually sipping coffee as if hanging out by the parking area was their normal morning ritual.

I sauntered over. "Something I can help you guys with?"

Jason rolled his eyes and tipped his head at Cole. "Sorry, but this one was dying to talk to you." I appreciated Jason coming along to rein Cole in.

Cole played coy. "I just wanted to see how everything went with the kitten."

I was just betting he did. "The kitten really likes Wesley. I smell an adoption in the air."

"Nice," Cole said. "So can I assume you helped Wesley with his... problem?" He smirked and inclined his head toward my t-shirt.

Jason whacked Cole on his arm. "Remember what we talked about? The boundaries thing?"

"What? I'm concerned about the kitten. The kitten problem." He wiggled his eyebrows.

I *tsked* at him just like my grandma used to. "You're better than that, Cole." I put my helmet on. "Don't give Wesley a hard time."

Too late, I realized the opening I'd given him.

Cole saw my chagrin and toasted me with his coffee cup. "I'm better than that, Keson."

Fucker. I got on my bike and rode away.

I took additional liberties with my work hours and knocked off early to shower and dress in the barn restroom. I'd considered getting ready at Wesley's cottage, but I was oddly into the whole *pick-him-up-at-the-front-door* scenario.

Underneath my date clothes were boxer briefs that displayed my dick to its best advantage. Among other things, Jake Lord was legendary for the size of his cock, and I wasn't going to be shown up.

I hoped Wesley had a plan for the date part of our evening, because I hadn't spared it a thought. I'd spent most of the day alternating between researching bees and imagining fucking Wesley.

As soon as I parked my truck and started up the walkway to the front porch, my mother called. I knew it was her even before I pulled the phone from my pocket. Not because she had a special ringtone, but because she had a sixth sense for when my brother and I were doing something we didn't want her to know about.

"Hey, Ma, I'm kinda busy." I paused before stepping onto the porch. Maybe I could get her off the phone before Wesley saw me. Nope, there he was.

"You're too busy to say hello to your old, neglected mother?"

I scoffed. "I spent all day Saturday with you. It's only Tuesday now."

"Hmm. What are you up to?"

At that moment, Wesley opened the door and said, "Hey— oops, sorry. I didn't know you were on the phone." He looked completely fuckable in faded jeans and a black button-up shirt that set off his eyes.

"Just a minute, Ma," I said, then pressed the phone to my chest like that would stop her from hearing me. "Sorry, I just need a sec."

He smiled, and I wanted to kiss him. Fuck, I was getting in over my head quick.

"Let me just make sure the kitten is locked up. I'll be right back."

I'd have to work fast to get my mother off the phone before Wesley returned. "Sorry, Ma. I've got a date."

"I see. What's his name?" And so the interrogation began.

"Wesley."

"Wesley. That's a good name. Where did you meet him?"

"Um, at the ranch." Shit, I hadn't sounded confident enough. She'd smell blood in the water.

"So he works with you?" Yep, I was in for it. And, to make things even better, Wesley came back outside.

"No, Ma. He's friends with Cole, Jason, and Will." I put my finger to my lips and then mouthed *Sorry* at Wesley. He looked amused.

Ma gasped. "Is he a celebrity?"

I closed my eyes and tilted my head back. "Ma, I really need to go."

"He *is* a celebrity. How exciting! Can you send me a picture?"

"Ma."

"I know, I know. You need to get going on your date. At least tell me, is this a real date, or just one of those hookups you're always having?"

I hung my head. I must have looked completely defeated because Wesley started rubbing circles on my back.

"It's a real date, Ma. I've—" Her squeal cut me off and I jerked the phone from my ear.

"You seal that deal, Keson," she yelled. "I need some grandbabies."

"Oh, my god, Ma." I couldn't even.

Wesley laughed, and then that fucker decided to spin my mother up even further. "Tell your mom I've already got a kid."

Ma let out another shriek. "What? How old? Boy or girl? When can I meet them?"

I narrowed my eyes at Wesley. He just stood there, grinning. His eyes sparkled with mirth. I could feel myself falling. *Fuck.*

"Laugh it up, asshole," I told him. My mother started complaining about my language, so I handed Wesley my phone and walked to the truck. *Get it together. He's just experimenting. This won't go anywhere.*

A few minutes later, Wesley climbed into the passenger side, still on the phone. "Yes, ma'am. That sounds lovely. I'll have to check my schedule though." My head whipped around in horror. She'd invited him over? What had I been thinking, giving him the phone?

"No, ma'am, not busy with work. I retired last year." He did *not* just say that to my mother. I put my hands over my mouth and stared at him, bug-eyed. He winked at me. "I'm fifty-five. Yes, ma'am."

Then he made a strangled laughing sound. "I'll have to ask him, but I hope so. Uh huh. Okay, I'll give you back to Keson so you can say goodbye."

"Bye, Ma. I'll talk to you tomorrow." Only if I can't avoid it.

"Oh, yes, you will." She paused. "I love you."

"Love you too." After we hung up, I leaned back in my seat, crossed my arms and glared at Wesley. "I was going to ease her into the whole age gap thing."

Unrepentant, Wesley rhapsodized, "Your mother is wonderful. She invited us for dinner sometime soon."

He paused, examining me, then seemed to realize something was wrong. "Um, is that not okay? Do you—I mean, I hoped we might keep seeing each other."

"Wesley. We're on our first date. I've *never* brought anyone home to meet my mother. If we go to dinner at her house, she's going to have us picking out wedding invitations." He didn't seem to find this as alarming as he should've. "And do I want to know what you told her you *have to ask me*?"

He lit up. "She wondered if you thought I was a silver fox."

I rolled my eyes. It could have been worse.

I put my key in the ignition, ready to get out of there. "Where are we going?"

"Um, if you don't mind driving into Austin, Will told me about a food truck park near a lake. And then we can go see a bunch of bats come out from under a bridge?"

"That's a great plan. I've never done that before. I'm in."

When I started the truck, KATE-FM was airing their news recap. Wouldn't you know, it was the story I least wanted to hear. I reached to turn it off, but Wesley stopped me. "Wait. I want to see how she's doing." The DJ read the PR rep's statement and Wesley frowned. "She's having more surgery? That doesn't bode well for the use of her hand." He shivered.

"That could've been me. It could've been anyone in the public eye."

I shook my head. "Her bodyguard dropped the ball. He wasn't looking where he should have been. He could've prevented it."

Wesley eyed me like I wasn't very bright. "Keson, I've been in crowds like that. People are trying to come at you from all sides. One bodyguard can't watch everyone."

I shook my head again but changed the subject. "Did Will tell you that bridge has the largest urban bat colony in the United States?"

———

The food trucks were as good as advertised, the lake was peaceful, and the massive cloud of bats was impressive. Wesley was charming and funny, and I was… not.

No, I was a walking, talking, bundle of tension. People, *strangers*, surrounded us. I was compelled to keep them all in view, to make sure none of them got close to Wesley.

Not that many were trying to. I'd been surprised when only a couple of people recognized him. I walked between Wesley and any groups, but even so, his face was fairly well known.

I knew I was being paranoid, so I tried to breathe and participate in our date. I listened to Wesley's rock and roll stories, and he told me how happy he felt about retiring. I told him my coming out story and about growing up around my parents' nursery business. I made a point to not look away from his face for minutes at a time.

But it was excruciating how much I wanted to. How much I needed to be on guard against possible threats.

Worst of all, Wesley could tell I wasn't solely focused on him. His smiles became smaller and dimmer as the night went on.

"You're not having a good time." My head whipped around from where I'd been staring at three senior citizens.

"I—" I couldn't deny it.

Wesley gave me a sad smile. "I understand." He stood up from the bench where we'd been sitting.

I stood up with him. "Wesley—"

"It's okay. I'm sure you're used to going clubbing and dancing all night. This," his hand swept around to encompass the bats and the bridge, "It's probably not something a young guy like you would do voluntarily."

I cocked my head, fully engaged in what he was saying for the first time since we'd gotten out of the truck. "How old do you think I am?"

He pursed his lips, then said, "Twenty-eight, maybe?"

I laughed. "My mother will be thrilled to hear that. No, I'm thirty-seven."

"What?" He appeared astonished. "You don't look it." I shrugged. Then his forehead crinkled. "But... your former job. I mean, no offense, but aren't you pretty old for... that?"

"You'd think so, but there are guys still at it who're your age. You've just got to keep in shape." I grinned and flexed my biceps for him. He blinked at me with his mouth open but didn't respond.

Okay then.

But I needed to answer his original statement. "I'm sorry I've been distracted. It's, um, well." I blew out a breath and looked around again before yanking my gaze back to Wesley.

"Did Cole tell you what happened at my last job? Why I'm spending quality time with plants and flowers instead of...." I shook my head, pressing my lips together. Wesley laid his hand on my arm. It was the first time he'd touched me since we'd been in public.

"He didn't," he said gently. "And you don't have to tell me unless you want to."

I managed not to scan the crowd again, instead looking only into Wesley's eyes. "It all went to shit so suddenly. I couldn't—"

"Oh, my *gahd*, are you, like, Jake Lord?" I spun around, backing against Wesley so I was between him and the threat.

The girl couldn't have been more than twenty. She appeared harmless enough, but the ten or more almost identical girls behind her made me extremely uneasy. I hadn't seen them approaching. How could I have missed them all in a pack like that? *Fuck.*

Wesley, kind as he was, stepped out from behind me to speak to the girl, but he kept one hand on my back the entire time. It helped, that touch. At least until I realized three of the eerily similar girls had their phones pointed at us. *Fuck, fuck, fuck.* Someone was going to notice Wesley's hand on me.

I turned to get his attention. He nodded, then flashed the girl a fake smile and excused us. We walked on as if people weren't recording every step we took.

"Does it bother you? People stopping me all the time?" Wesley sounded worried.

"What? It's your life. I understand." Maybe he wouldn't notice I hadn't answered his question.

"Okay, but if it does start to bother you, will you tell me? The constant attention can be a lot." He sort of puffed up. "I have some great disguises though."

I smiled, but I knew it looked strained. "Let's head home."

I was glad of the darkness as I blinked back tears. I was in no shape mentally to date Wesley. I didn't know how I'd ever thought I could be.

I'd only known him for twenty-four hours, but I knew I was going to miss him for much, much longer.

CHAPTER 5
WESLEY

KESON WAS QUIET ON THE DRIVE HOME. I WANTED TO CIRCLE back to what he'd started to tell me about his former job, but if he wasn't volunteering the story, it wasn't any of my business.

I was pretty sure, though, that he didn't want me. He didn't want *us*.

I knew it was too much to have expectations on our first date, but I really, really liked him. And wanted him. Damn, did I want him. I wanted *us*.

I had nothing to lose, so I thought I might as well ask. We were exiting the highway for Bent Oak, so I was running out of time.

I cleared my throat. "It wasn't just my choice of date activity, was it? You're having second thoughts about dating me at all."

Keson grimaced. "I'm sorry." He took one hand off the steering wheel to run it rapidly up and down his thigh. "I really like you, Wesley." Then he went silent.

I folded my arms like a pouting toddler. "Weren't you the one joking about saying *it's not me, it's you*?"

He sighed, his whole body collapsing back into the seat. I hadn't realized how tense he'd been. "I mentioned my old job ended really badly."

"Right." I held up my hands. "You don't have to tell me if it's difficult for you." I deliberately let my hands fall to my lap instead of crossing my arms again.

Keson didn't look away from the road ahead. "It's just too much right now. I didn't realize how it was affecting me until we were out together. Doing *that*, even if it's not for, like, a job…. With you, with *anyone*…." He shuddered.

Oh, fuck. I was a tool. An utter, fucking, unfeeling asshole. Christ, Wesley, you didn't even consider what kind of experience would put someone off a career as a sex worker!

"Keson, I'm so sorry. I didn't think about…."

"I know, Wesley, I do. I didn't think about it either, actually, though I should've. Jason's been trying to talk me into seeing somebody. Like a therapist." He snorted. "I kept blowing him off."

"You're going to go now?"

"Yeah."

"Good for you."

We didn't have much to say to each other after that.

———

Even the kitten purring on my pillow the next morning didn't improve my mood.

"At least you got a decent night's sleep," I groused, even though my lack of sleep and my bad mood weren't the kitten's fault.

In a few hours, Freddy would pick me up and take me back to the condo I was renting in downtown Austin. Back to real life. I wasn't ready to leave the ranch. I loved it here; no one expected me to be or act a certain way just because I was famous. I felt like Cole, Jason, and Will could become good friends.

And then there was Keson.

I felt awful for him, suffering PTSD or whatever effects he was experiencing from his recent trauma. I was also feeling sad for myself, not being able to date Keson and get to know him better. We hadn't spent that much time together, but we had amazing chemistry. In my entire life I hadn't been that hard after merely making out with someone.

And it wasn't just that he was a man. If I pictured kissing one of my actor crushes, previously my favorite jerk-off fodder, it wasn't nearly as riveting as the thought of kissing Keson again.

But his trauma meant sex was too triggering for him. Maybe therapy would help, but it might not.

I sat up in the bed. Sex wasn't the be-all, end-all of a relationship, though, was it? Okay, I could admit that for almost all of my past relationships—if you could call them that—sex had been the instigating factor, as well as the primary way my lovers and I had created intimacy with each other.

But that wasn't the type of intimacy I was looking for this time. I wanted a partner, someone to come home to each day, someone to share all the little ups and downs of life with.

Could I be satisfied with a relationship where sex was completely off the table? What if he couldn't have sex for years? What if he could never have sex again?

I'd known the man for less than forty-eight hours. Even if *I* was willing to see if a non-sexual romantic relationship might work between us, would Keson even consider it? I wouldn't want him to feel like there was any pressure to "fix" himself so we could have sex.

Hoping coffee would help with my deliberations, I trudged to the kitchen. The kitten trotted behind and meowed for its breakfast. I started the coffee and dutifully poured fresh kibble and water into the bowls, then I scooped the litter box.

The coffee was almost ready when my phone rang. It wasn't even 7:00am yet. Before I could say more than hello, Cole started talking. "Hey, sorry to call so early, but I didn't want to interrupt your date last night."

"It's fine."

"Oh, good. I kind of felt like a creeper waiting for your lights to go on, so sorry if that was weird." I smiled. The Cole I'd met here, the one I'd gone riding with yesterday, was a far cry from the friendly-but-reserved movie star I'd met several years ago.

"It's not weird; don't worry about it."

"Right. So, is there any way you can stay another day? Or can your son pick you up tonight instead of this morning?"

My crappy mood lifted a little. "I'd love to stay longer. I don't *have* to leave today; I just thought two nights would be short enough not to overstay my welcome."

"Great! Please stay." Cole's tone rose with excitement. "We have an appointment at one o'clock."

"We do? What for?"

Cole paused. "You know, I think I'll let it be a surprise. Come up to the house for lunch around noon and we'll leave from here. I can't wait to hear about your date!"

My mood soured again. I *hmmmed* then said goodbye and ended the call. I immediately texted Freddy to tell him I was staying another day. He gave me a thumbs up and said he'd come get me tomorrow instead.

I looked down at the kitten. "We have a few hours to kill. What do you say we find out if you like guitar music?"

————

At lunch I managed to dance around Cole's interest in last night's date. I'd planned my strategy in advance, arriving armed with questions about how he liked living in Bent Oak. That worked like a charm, and he was easily distracted.

My choice of topics was fortuitous since the surprise appointment turned out to be a tour of a house just going on the market. The property boasted five acres, with a big house and a barn.

It backed right up to the Triple the Love Ranch

"If you don't buy it, we will," Jason told me. "But since you're looking anyway, we might as well give you the first shot at it. We'd love to have you as a neighbor." My heart warmed at that statement; they'd only known me for a few days.

It'd been ages since I'd had real friends. Friends I didn't work with, who didn't want anything from me. I was almost ready to sign the contract sight unseen.

The owner was getting on in years and couldn't live alone anymore. His grandson, Neill, was a real estate agent and had approached the three of them with the opportunity to purchase it. Neill had shown us around and waited patiently while Cole did his selling job for him.

"And," Cole told me as he dragged me to the second floor of the house, "You can see where this property meets ours back there." He pointed out the window at an enormous mass of trees. I knew Cole had installed a fence, but I couldn't see it. I liked knowing paparazzi and fans couldn't get at the house from that direction. "We could put in a gate and a road so we could go back and forth between our houses without driving around on the public streets." That did sound appealing.

The property needed work. The house, a huge Victorian, seemed to have last been updated in the seventies. The barn sagged a little on one side. The grounds were completely overgrown. Maybe Keson would tell me which plants were weeds and which weren't.

I imagined Keson walking the land with me, pointing out what plants to remove and what to keep. Helping me decide how to renovate the place. Coming home from his work at the ranch each night to cuddle with me on the couch. Eating breakfast together every morning.

Sex be damned, I wanted that. Or, at the very least, I wanted to take a shot at it. Maybe Keson and I would work out; maybe we wouldn't. But If I didn't try, I'd never know.

"What do you think?" Cole nudged me.

"I'm buying it."

And as soon as we got back to the ranch, I was going to find Keson.

CHAPTER 6
KESON

WORK WAS SUPPOSED TO TAKE MY MIND OFF WESLEY. BUT I hadn't been able to shake the regret and disappointment on his face when I'd said I couldn't be with him. When was the last time someone had been that interested in spending time with me? Sure, I'd had relationships, but none of them had had this kind of burning attraction.

Maybe if I dealt with my issues I'd be in a good enough headspace where I could be with him.

That goal, more than Jason prodding me, more than my vague acknowledgement of the necessity, gave me the kick in the ass I needed to do something.

After I dropped my plan for the beehives and honey production on Arturo's desk, I headed for the main house. I slowed as I neared the guest cottage. The Triumph was still out front. I'd thought Wesley had planned to leave that morning, but I could hear him playing the guitar and singing.

I paused by some lantana bushes that would hide my presence if he were near the front windows. I was making a habit of eavesdropping on Wesley, but once again I couldn't help myself.

I recognized an old Book of Love song that KATE-FM played frequently. Except when Wesley got to the chorus, he substituted "noses" for the song's original "roses" and then made a *boop* sound. I heard the kitten meow and Wesley laughed before starting to play again.

Crap, he was singing to the fucking kitten. Could he be more adorable?

With renewed purpose I walked quickly past the cottage and wound around to the back door of the ranch house. Tracey and Will were both sitting with their laptops at the kitchen table.

They greeted me, and I steeled myself. "Hey, Will, can I talk to you for a minute?"

"Sure," he said. "I could use a break. Let's go out on the deck."

Once outside, I lowered my voice. I knew how sound carried out here. "Um, I wanted to ask you…. Jason said you've got a therapist? Can I get their contact info?"

———

I'd just finished my after-work shower and was heading out to my bike when Wesley walked into the barn. I wasn't expecting him, and my heart and my brain did a complicated dance of *Yes, we like him!* and *No, he needs more than we can give!* while my mouth just fell open in surprise.

Wesley gave me a quick, tentative smile. "Hey. Um, can I talk to you?"

I hugged my backpack to my chest. "Sure."

"Right." He rubbed his hand over his jaw, then straightened his spine. "I've done a lot of thinking today. I like you. A lot.

And, as I said before, I'm looking for more than sex. I want a partner, someone to come home to, to spend time with."

"Okaaay," I said, because he seemed to be waiting for some sort of response.

Wesley nodded. "I know you've got, um, things to work through. And I'd like to be there for you while you do that." He held up his hand to stop me from speaking, even though I hadn't started to. I was far too invested in what he was going to say next. "No pressure for sex." My brows beetled and I tilted my head, but he carried on. "I mean, if you'll allow it, I'd like to hold your hand and kiss you occasionally, but I want to try a relationship with you. Even if it means no sex at all, for now or even forever."

I reared my head back. *"What?"* I couldn't find any other words.

He nodded again, like he'd expected my response. "You might think it's a lot to ask of someone, but, Keson, you're not *asking* me to do this. I'm offering. All I want is to be with you."

Wesley's phone started to ring.

"Wait, I don't—"

He held up a finger. "Sorry, let me tell Freddy I'll call him back."

I subsided as he answered the phone. What the fuck was he talking about, no sex?

Suddenly Wesley's entire body went absolutely rigid. *"What?"* He listened some more. "Where are you?" Then, "I'm coming right now."

He hung up the phone and reached for me, his eyes wild and

his body swaying. "Freddy's in the hospital. He was in a car accident. He broke his arm and he might have a concussion."

I swung my backpack over one shoulder, grasped his elbow and turned him toward the exit. "I've got the truck. I'll drive you."

"Okay," he whispered.

———

I dropped Wesley at the emergency entrance, and by the time I came back from parking the truck, he'd already been taken to see Mac.

"Who are you here to visit?" the *I-have-no-fucks-left-to-give* intake nurse demanded impatiently.

"Um, Freddy—or he goes by Mac—um... Lord?" It dawned on me I had no idea what Wesley's real last name was.

The nurse typed on her keyboard, then said, "Bed eight. Security has to escort you."

A security guard asked to see my ID. I was given a visitor pass, and he scanned his badge to let me through some automatic doors.

I turned a corner just in time to see Mac being wheeled out by a nurse with Wesley following behind. I jogged to catch up.

Wesley gave me a wan smile. "They're moving him to a room. He's staying overnight for observation because of his head injury."

I put my hand on Wesley's back. He gave me a startled glance, then smiled a little brighter. I would've rather held his hand, but we were in public and we hadn't discussed it.

When the elevator doors opened, the nurse turned Mac's chair around and backed him in.

"Oh, hey. Keson, right?"

"Yeah. Hi, Mac. I'm sorry to hear about your accident."

Mac made a face. His mother had been some sort of supermodel, but Mac's features were just a more finely honed version of his dad's.

"This was not on my list of things to do today," Mac complained. "Stupid drunk college students."

"Is the other driver okay?"

Mac rolled his eyes and nodded. "Not a scratch on him or his drunk buddies."

We exited the elevator. The nurse led us to Mac's room and then spent what Mac seemed to feel was an overlong amount of time getting him settled and educated on how to use the call button and bed controls.

As soon as the door shut behind the nurse, Mac rounded on me. "Keson, dare I hope you're here as Dad's date and not as a bodyguard?"

"Um." I shot Wesley a desperate glance, but he just looked confused. "We had a date but…." I shrugged, holding out my hands.

"Freddy," Wesley said hotly. "Keson's not a bodyguard." Mac opened his mouth but Wesley barreled on. "He may have more muscles than I do, but that doesn't mean he has to watch out for me. He's my… I mean, we're seeing each other. Or trying to."

That was a nice sentiment from Wesley, but I was the one who was confused now. "Did you just say I'm not a bodyguard?"

"Yeah?"

Mac and I both gave him puzzled looks.

I knew Wesley hadn't recognized me when we met, but had I ever explicitly told him what my job had been? I'd said I couldn't be with him because of…. Holy shit, I hadn't said anything specific. I flashed back to Wesley saying we didn't have to have sex to be together. Surely he didn't think…? How the hell would he have come to that conclusion?

I took his hand. "Wesley, what do you think my job was before I started doing groundskeeping at the ranch?"

Wesley opened his mouth, then looked worriedly between me and Mac. "It's okay," I told him. "You think I was doing sex work?"

"Yes?"

"Oh, my god, Dad, you thought Keson was an escort?"

I flapped my hand at Mac to hush him.

Wesley's face became even paler. "Is that wrong? But, you… Cole said…." He leaned his head back and looked at the ceiling. "I told Cole I was bisexual but I'd never been with a man —sorry, Freddy." Mac waved him on. "Um, then Cole said something about it being too bad they didn't know any escorts. Then he shouted your name and wondered if you'd be willing." He shrugged helplessly.

I started to chuckle as I went over our past conversations. Wesley's face was bright red, so I pulled him into a hug. "It's okay, Wesley." Then I laughed. And laughed some more. "Your face," I wheezed. "That's why you were making that face when I told you how old some of my colleagues are."

Mac guffawed, then grabbed his head. He hadn't been

allowed any prescription pain meds because of the concussion. Wesley released me and went to his side.

"I'd better leave you two alone so Mac can get some rest." Wesley turned to protest, but I shook my head. "There's someone else here I need to visit. I'll be back." I hesitated. "Actually, Wesley, can I talk to you real quick?" I looked over at Mac. "Just one more thing I need to clear up."

Mac grinned. "I bet. This is going to make the best story to tell at your wedding."

Wesley's eyes went wide. I grabbed his hand and pulled him into the attached bathroom. I shut the door on the sound of Mac's wolf whistle, then I shoved Wesley up against the wall and kissed him as if my life depended on it.

"You," I pulled back just barely enough to whisper against his lips, "You thought I was a sex worker, and not only did you ask me on a date, but you were willing to give up sex to be with me?" I pressed my groin to his. We both groaned.

"I thought," Wesley panted into my mouth, "You were having PTSD from a bad sexual experience."

I couldn't help myself. I gathered him in and hugged him. "You are way too wonderful for the likes of me, but I've decided I'm keeping you anyway."

"Yeah?"

"Yeah." I kissed him again. "For the record, I was a bodyguard, like Mac said. That was the issue I had on our date. Being in public with you. I was constantly worried about your safety, even though there was no threat."

Wesley gently cupped my face. "Poppy?" he asked, searching my eyes.

"Poppy," I confirmed. I leaned my forehead against his. "She was wearing a disguise because of the stalker. I would've been plenty of protection if her fucking PA hadn't posted that photo. There were just too many people, and my backup couldn't get there in time."

"She doesn't blame you, does she?"

I stood upright and tried to straighten Wesley's rumpled clothes. "I'm about to find out."

CHAPTER 7
WESLEY

I RETURNED TO FREDDY'S BEDSIDE AND PULLED THE GUEST CHAIR over. He let me hold his hand, which wasn't something he'd allowed since he'd turned thirteen.

"I could have lost you today." I pressed my forehead down on our joined hands. I was so glad I'd already decided to move here. People were home, not places.

"Dad, the accident wasn't that bad. I'm fine. At least, I will be," he said in his most reassuring voice. I nodded against our hands, then I made myself sit up. Freddy didn't comment when I wiped my eyes on my sleeve.

"I put an offer on a house today," I told him. He let me go on and on about the property and my plans for renovating it. Then, when my guard was down, he pounced. I kept forgetting he'd been to law school.

"Tell me about Keson," he demanded. "No, wait. First, tell me how you didn't recognize him when his face has been in every news story about the attack on that pop star. I recognized him when I dropped you off on Monday."

I shrugged. "Photos like that, where someone is injured or in distress, are an invasion of privacy. I wouldn't want to be the subject of them, so I try not to look."

Freddy nodded thoughtfully. "There's going to be a media shitstorm when somebody realizes you're dating a guy."

"I know. I need to talk to Keson about it. I'm thinking of hiring a bodyguard from the company he worked for. Maybe knowing the people who'll be watching out for us will ease his concerns, and it'll keep the photographers at a distance."

Freddy and I continued to chat. In some ways it was a more intimate conversation than we'd had in years. Freddy did text his mother about his accident, but she lived in Europe so she wouldn't be rushing to his bedside. His friend Tobias called and, since I didn't have a car, Freddy arranged for Tobias to pick him up the next day once he was released.

The nurse came in with Freddy's dinner. When he finished eating, he seemed tired. I was getting ready to leave when Keson stuck his head around the door. "Can I bring a guest to visit?"

I looked at Freddy, and he shrugged so I told Keson to come on in.

Keson backed out and a young woman in a wheelchair preceded him into the room. Freddy, who'd been raised around celebrities of all kinds, sucked in a breath.

Poppy waved her bandaged right hand. I didn't think I'd ever seen a photo of her without make-up. She was still beautiful, but she looked frail and worn. "Hi, there. Sorry to barge in like this. I was going stir crazy in my room, so I strong-armed Keson into bringing me down here."

"I don't blame you a bit. It's nice to meet you. I'm Wesley, in case Keson didn't tell you. This is my son, Fr—er, Mac."

Poppy raised an eyebrow at my almost-slip but didn't say anything. She rolled herself over to Freddy's bedside and they compared arm injuries. I took the opportunity to move closer to Keson.

He leaned against me, and I put my arm around his waist. I could get used to holding him. "How did it go?"

He sighed. "Good. I should've gone to see her before now."

"Not if you weren't ready. You went through some trauma too, remember?"

"Yeah, I know," he grumbled. I pressed a kiss to his temple, and out of the corner of my eye I saw Freddy and Poppy watching us. They put their heads together and started whispering. Keson said, "I told Poppy you and I were dating. I hope that's okay."

I smiled. "That's fantastic."

Just then Poppy squealed, "What? No way! That's legit bad-ass!" Was Freddy *blushing*?

"What's bad-ass?" Keson asked.

"Mac's real name!" She beamed, looking between Freddy and us.

Keson blinked. "Wesley calls him Freddy."

Poppy gasped. "You don't *know*?"

I cocked my head, thinking back. "I guess it hasn't come up. His name—"

"*No!*" Poppy threw her unbandaged hand in the air like a school crossing guard. She turned and batted her eyes at Freddy. "We should make a bet. Or a prize for Keson if he figures it out. Like, give him a deadline."

Keson raised an eyebrow. "You're on. Terms?"

Freddy was too dazzled by Poppy's attention, or maybe his concussion, to come up with any ideas, so I tossed out, "If Keson hasn't figured out Freddy's full name in one year, then he has to create a landscape design for a property of Freddy's choosing." Keson's head whipped around to me.

Poppy sat up straight in her wheelchair. She looked vibrant in a way she hadn't when she'd arrived. "Yes! That's perfect. Keson, the way you talk about your gardening work, it's like it's what you were meant to do."

Keson shrugged and shifted his feet. "And if I figure it out?"

Poppy and Freddy looked to me again. "Um, if you figure it out before the deadline, Poppy has to dedicate a song to you on her next album."

Poppy looked down at her bandaged hand. "If there's going to be a next album." Freddy touched her shoulder without saying anything. Where had he learned to be so thoughtful?

"Poppy," I said in a no-nonsense tone, "I don't know what the prognosis is for your hand, but you *will* make another album. Hell, I'd be happy to play on it if you can't."

Her eyes flew up to meet mine. "Really?" she whispered.

"Really." *Fuck*, I'd just adopted another stray. Now I had both a kitten and a pop princess to take care of.

"Then I agree," she proclaimed.

Keson frowned. "I'm in, obviously. But it seems too easy. Surely I could just Google Mac's real name?"

"No!" I thought Poppy was going to stand up out of her wheelchair. "You have to promise, no Googling. No internet searches, no computer hacking. IRL methods only."

Keson twisted his mouth for a moment then brightened. "Oh, like bribery. I can do that." He wiggled his eyebrows at me.

"Bring it on," I told him, making Mac and Poppy snicker. Then I saw my chance. "Well, it might not matter anyway. Mac wants to change his name before he takes the bar exam." Freddy glared at me while Poppy expressed her disapproval.

I smiled serenely. Keson elbowed me and whispered, "Damn, you're good."

Then Keson cleared his throat. "Hey, I'm going to take Wesley home. Poppy, Del's right outside, so whenever you're ready to leave, he can take you back to your room."

We all said our goodbyes. On the way out Keson introduced me to Del, his roommate and coworker at Shelton Security.

Before I could finish greeting the man, I found myself being hustled along the hallway to the elevator. "Are we in a hurry?"

"Yes," Keson snapped out.

"Okay. Why?"

The elevator doors opened. Keson urged me inside, and as soon as the doors shut again, he crowded me against the wall. "I'm taking you back to the cottage, and we're going to have sex."

When the elevator opened on the ground floor, I was the one leading the way to Keson's truck.

―――

I put my hand on Keson's thigh and left it there the entire drive back to the cottage. It wasn't my fault if he dressed right.

"Do you want something to eat?" I asked him as he parked.

"Later." Keson, I'd discovered, became a man of few words when he was horny.

He chivvied me out of the truck and into the house. The kitten meowed at us from the kitchen, but we went straight to the bedroom.

When we finally reached the bed, Keson put his hand on my neck. "Are you good with this?"

"Oh, yes. I mean, I don't know if I'm up for, um, *everything*."

Keson grinned and winked. "Remember, if you can't say it out loud, you aren't ready to do it."

"Fuck off. You know what I mean. Anal. I'm not ready for anal." I could feel myself blushing. "I'm not, um, prepped." See, I could say it.

Keson kissed me, just a quick peck. He was still grinning. "No worries. I figure since this is your first time cock-to-cock, as it were, we'll have plenty to keep us occupied without anal."

Something inside me relaxed. I definitely wanted to try it, but Keson was right. Tonight I'd rather we learned each other's bodies and shared where we liked to be touched.

Without ceremony, Keson pulled off his shirt. Then he winked at me and ever-so-slowly inched down his zipper. He wasn't wearing any underwear. Holy shit, *he wasn't wearing any underwear*.

So far I could only see his treasure trail and the top of his pubic hair. And muscles. I swallowed. The man was ripped.

Keson pushed his pants down and toed them off with his shoes. I licked my lips, which made me notice I was breathing through my mouth.

Keson's cock—his thick, beautiful cock—was fully hard. He

ran the tips of his fingers up and down his shaft. I'd never been this close to another man's erection.

"Wesley."

"Huh?" I couldn't stop staring. At the precome pearling from his tip. At his balls hanging below. What would they feel like?

I vaguely registered Keson chuckling again. "Wesley, you need to take your clothes off."

"Um. Right." Clothes off. Yes, I could do that. I just had to look at Keson a little bit longer.

"Here, why don't I help you?" Keson reached for the hem of my t-shirt. I let him pull it over my head, and I instinctively ran my palms down the underside of his arms, then across his pecs. Holy shit, I was touching another man. More importantly, I was touching Keson.

He unzipped my pants and shoved them to the floor. I had to stop everything to get my feet out of my boots, but as quick as I could I was upright again, wearing only my boxers.

"Where was I?" I smoothed my hands over Keson's abs, then his hips. His pupils were wide, and his breathing heavy. His hands, bigger and more calloused than those of any lover I'd had before, held my biceps like he didn't intend to let go.

The corner of my mouth lifted. I might be inexperienced with men, and I might be older, but he wanted me.

"I'm going to kiss you now," I told him. I received a smile in response, so I stepped into Keson's body, putting my feet between his. I leaned down, but then—

Holy hell!

My breath stopped as Keson's dick slid against my own. I was taller, so we didn't align exactly, but it was enough. My boxers were no barrier. In the thousands of sexual encounters over my lifetime, I'd never felt anything like this. I stood there, pressed against Keson from my thighs to my open mouth. I wasn't even kissing him. My lips hovered against his as we panted together.

I needed to do something, to move, to kiss Keson. But I didn't want to risk losing the sensation of our dicks pressed against each other, so I did nothing.

Keson smiled against my mouth, and my lips curled up to answer. "Sorry," I muttered, not moving my head back even a millimeter to make room for speech. "I got distracted."

He grinned wider. "I could tell."

Keson pulled me tighter into his body, and I shoved my mouth onto his, now desperate to taste him. The heat of his mouth, the slide of his tongue combined with the feel of his cock next to mine was overwhelming.

I cried out when Keson pushed me away. "What's wrong?"

Keson's eyes crinkled. "Nothing at all. Just, before we go any further I want you to know I'm negative and I'm on PrEP."

"I'm not on PrEP, but I'm negative too. I haven't been with anyone since my last test."

Keson made an approving hum. He nodded toward my boxers. "You need to lose those."

I smirked and shoved the boxers to the floor in one smooth move. I'd had a lot of practice, after all.

I put my hands on my hips to frame my most impressive asset. Keson lifted his eyebrows. "Well, damn, I guess the rumors about Jake Lord's giant dick are true."

"Wesley," I corrected.

"Wesley Lord's dick then," he said agreeably. Then he hesitated. "Wait, is Lord even your real last name?"

I snorted. "It's Gaylord."

"*Gay*lord. Wow. Wow. The jokes. How do I pick just one?"

"Ha ha." I tried to shove him back toward the bed, but he was immovable. Fuck, those muscles. I ran my hands over his shoulders.

"And what's your middle name, Wesley Gaylord?" He tweaked my left nipple and a bolt of lust shot to my balls. As if I wasn't hard enough already. *Fuck.*

"Not to be rude, but can we have this discussion later?"

Keson smirked and tweaked my right nipple. I almost doubled over. "You're trying to change the subject. Spill. What is it?"

"Ugh, it's Dwain." I spelled it.

Keson chuckled. "Wow," he said again. "I hope you were nicer to Mac than your parents were to you."

I reached out and twisted Keson's nipple hard, something I'd never have dared to do to a woman. "I'll never tell."

Keson casually reached out and cupped my balls. I widened my legs, and something resembling a whimper left my mouth. "Oh, you'll tell me," Keson promised. At least he was breathing as heavily as I was.

Keson palmed my ass, but he still kept up the conversation through his panting. "But Freddy got Lord for his last name?"

"Yeah, since Freddy's mother let me choose his first and middle name, it was only fair she pick his last name. She chose Lord."

"Ah, you've given me a clue. You chose Mac's secret name." He ran his fingers through my crack, the tips brushing across my hole. My breath caught, and I found myself leaning against his broad chest.

"Fuck, Keson."

He smiled into my collarbone, but he didn't remove his hand from my ass. I levered myself upright, then I watched Keson's face as he tracked my hands moving down his body. When I got near his groin, he snatched my wrists and held them out and away. "If you touch my cock, I'm going to come."

My body flooded with triumph and satisfaction. I'd done that. I'd turned Keson on to the point of losing control.

"Is that why we've been having this stupid conversation for so long?"

He laughed. "Busted. I've been about to blow since you dropped your pants."

"No more talking. I'm about to touch another man's dick for the first time." The dick in question twitched. I twisted my wrists to break out of his hold and he didn't resist.

Barely breathing, I reached one hand for his dick and the other for his balls. I'm an overachiever like that.

Keson's grunt when I grasped him, his moan, instantly demolished any lingering insecurity inside me. This was sex. The mechanics might be slightly different, but this was still something I was good at. Keson could take the lead this time, but I'd make sure he'd have one of the most explosive orgasms of his life.

Keson's balls were big. Hot, heavy, and full. They felt, well, pretty much like mine, to be honest. And he seemed to favor the same gentle rolling massage I liked. I'd have to get my mouth on those bad boys soon.

I'd been relieved to see Keson's cock was shorter than mine and not quite as thick. People always told me how great it must be to have a big dick. Personally, I'd have preferred a smaller one. Mine was difficult for most of my partners to take. Keson's wasn't as intimidating, though. I couldn't wait to get my lips around it, and my ass too one day.

Taking Keson's cock and balls in my hands felt like coming home. I couldn't decide if I was angry I'd waited all these years to try sex with a man, or if I was glad I'd held out so that man would be Keson.

I stroked him, trying out a little twist and squeeze I always enjoyed. His, "Oh, yeah, just like that," was all the validation I needed.

His balls tightened in my hand, and his dick got even stiffer. Smiling to myself, I released him completely. I ignored his protests and pushed him toward the bed.

"We need to get horizontal." I yanked the quilt off then waved him forward.

Keson narrowed his eyes at me. "And here I was, being all nice and gentle with you since it's your first time with a dude. I'm not holding back after this."

"I can handle it," I assured him. "Now get on the bed."

Muttering under his breath, he did as I'd instructed, but at the last second he captured one of my hands and yanked me with him. Stumbling forward, I tripped and fell on top of Keson in a gangly heap of arms and legs. Keson clasped my chest and groin to his, then rolled us so he was on top.

Then he took my mouth.

This time, Keson's kiss was forceful and demanding. He ground his hips against mine and I moaned as our cocks rubbed against each other. I was grateful he'd taken charge of the kiss since I couldn't control any of my muscles—all my focus was on that sweet, sweet friction. I briefly remembered my intention to give Keson a mind-blowing orgasm, but at that moment I couldn't do more than clutch his shoulders.

And when Keson grasped both our cocks together in one hand? My eyes rolled back in my head and I came.

I clasped him to me as he sought his own orgasm. He only needed a few more pulls, my cum easing the slide of his fist. His body clenched and bowed for several seconds, which made me feel like I'd won a prize. When he was done, I hugged him until the cum and sweat between our bodies was too uncomfortable to ignore.

I rolled so Keson slid off me and we lay facing each other. His eyes crinkled and his lips curled up in a satisfied smirk. "So, how did I do, popping your gay cherry?"

I hitched up one shoulder. "Eh, it was alright. I could see myself trying it again one day." I leaned forward and gave him the most blistering kiss I could manage.

When we came up for air, Keson pulled away from me with a grimace. "I think we need a shower."

"Too much work. Stay right there." I peeled myself away from him—okay, he had a point about the shower, but I really just wanted to go to sleep. I shuffled to the bathroom and came back with a couple of damp towels. The top sheet wasn't too messy, so after I got Keson cleaned off, I tugged it out from under him and spread it over us.

He turned to lie on his side, then he tucked me against his body and wrapped his arm around my waist. Another first for the night. I'd never been anyone's little spoon before.

I liked it. I liked *Keson*.

A wave of emotion—a heady mixture of anticipation, excitement, and hope—shivered through me. I'd felt this same way on the day I'd landed my first record deal. I'd felt it when I found out Freddy's mother was pregnant. And now I felt it with Keson.

I wasn't naïve; me being with Keson would bring a media spotlight on our lives, and I'd have to be careful of his anxiety about my safety.

But if he was willing to weather that storm with me, I'd endure almost anything. He'd be worth it. Our life together would be worth it.

I couldn't wait.

EPILOGUE

KESON

THE GARDEN WAS AS BEAUTIFUL AS I'D PLANNED IT TO BE, JUST IN time for the wedding. The plants and shrubs would be much more lush in a few years, but it was still the garden sanctuary I'd envisioned. I loved the scent of honeysuckle drifting across the pool, attracting bees and butterflies. A gentle breeze rustled through the oaks and pines.

Something was off.

The guests had started to trickle in and were seating themselves in the chairs Wesley and I had arranged on the deck. The huge pergola and the deck underneath had been the first thing I'd told Wesley he needed, especially once he mentioned the pool and an outdoor kitchen. The spaces between the overhead beams were wide enough to let sunlight through but narrow enough to prevent the various media helicopters from photographing what they no doubt hoped would be some salacious man-on-man activities. I snorted to myself. Some photographers had undoubtedly gotten some partial shots, especially after I'd moved in eight months ago, but as far as I was aware, nothing had ever been published.

I reached out and patted one of the posts. So far the media hadn't gotten wind of today's wedding, but if they did, our trusty pergola would foil any unauthorized photos.

All was going to plan, but I just couldn't shake an uneasy feeling.

"Stand down and stop scanning the crowd like you're on duty. Everything's fine." I was sure Del's hand on my shoulder was meant to be reassuring, but all it did was ramp my foreboding up a notch.

"Bruh, I know you mean well, but something's up. Half these people don't belong here."

"I cleared all the guests. Relax." He patted me again then dropped his hand.

I glared at him. "I'm not being paranoid." He opened his mouth, but I pointed a finger to stop him. "Don't you dare mention calling my therapist. I'm not wrong." Some days were better than others, but therapy had really helped me manage my anxiety when I was out in public with Wesley. This was different, though. It wasn't anxiety telling me the guest list didn't make sense.

Case in point. "Keson!" My parents and brother came over to give me hugs. I mean, I supposed you could say my mom and dad were Mac's unofficial grandparents, but they'd only met a couple of times. For a wedding this small it was odd for them to be invited. Which is exactly what I pointed out to Del as soon as they left to find seats.

Tracey was expected. She was now Poppy's PA since Cole didn't need her as much anymore. But was Arturo here as her plus one? They were friends, sure, but were they that close?

Mac's mother and her husband were here, of course. I'd been prepared to dislike Marcella, but she was warm and funny, and she genuinely seemed happy that Wesley and I were together.

On the other side of Marcella sat Cole, Jason, and Will. Poppy had stayed in their guest cottage while she'd recovered from her surgeries, so of course they'd been invited.

I nudged Del. "What's Brian doing here?" He was Jason's brother, along with being Del and my old boss at Shelton Security. With Brian's blessing, Poppy had hired Del away from Shelton to be her personal head of security.

Mal and Spence were running event security, but Brian was sitting next to Will and holding a glass of champagne. He was a guest.

Del shrugged. "Not sure. I wasn't consulted on who got invited."

Before I could ask exactly who else was coming, we were interrupted by Mac and Poppy, along with Tobias. Mac's best friend and law partner was performing the ceremony.

I hugged all of them and congratulated Mac and Poppy on their big day.

"You know, Keson," Mac started. His voice held a mischievous tone I'd learned to be wary of. "It's been just over a year since we made that bet."

"Bet?" I asked disingenuously. I knew exactly what bet he was talking about. I'd just been acting like I'd forgotten for the past twelve months.

"You know, the bet we made in my hospital room that you couldn't figure out my real name."

"Oh, that bet. Right."

Mac elbowed Tobias. "Since you haven't figured it out yet, we decided to keep the mystery alive, and Tobias isn't going to use my real name in the ceremony." He chortled while Poppy and Tobias rolled their eyes.

I gave Mac a pitying look. "You're assuming I didn't find out your real name within a month of the bet, *Freddy Mercury Lord*." Mac and Poppy gasped, but Tobias laughed. "I thought about telling you, but I was going to design whatever landscaping you wanted anyway." I smirked. "And you were having *so* much fun trying to keep it from me."

Mac demanded, "How the hell did you find out?"

I grinned, showing all my teeth. "You were too focused on getting into Poppy's pants to think about where you were leaving your wallet, *Freddy*. You forgot Poppy's head of security is my best friend."

Mac gasped in outrage. "*Et tu*, Del?" He glared over my shoulder where Del was taking cover.

Poppy intervened. "Keson, bet or no bet, I've already written the dedications for my new album, and your name is front and center."

"What? Why? That's not—"

"It's what I wanted, and it's my fucking album."

"But, I—"

"Don't you dare argue with me on my wedding day!" We stared each other down, both of us with hands on hips. Then we simultaneously laughed and hugged.

"Fine, have it your way."

"Always," she crowed.

"Okay, we need to get ready," Tobias steered Mac and Poppy toward the area where the ceremony was to take place. Poppy had elected not to walk down the aisle, stating she'd rather they stood together as equals from the start.

Wesley trotted up, out of breath and slightly disheveled. Damn, I wished *I'd* mussed him up like that. Maybe we could sneak away during the reception.

"Are they ready?" he panted.

"Yes, what's up? Why are you all...." I gestured up and down at him.

"I couldn't find Twinkie. I wanted to lock her in our bedroom so she'd be safe."

I channeled my grandma and *tsked,* then started straightening his clothing and taming his hair. "Where was she?"

Wesley huffed, "In our closet sleeping on my black sweater. I must have looked in there five times."

I kissed the corner of his mouth. "There, now you don't look like you've been searching under the beds for your damn cat."

"She's *our* cat."

"Uh huh. Sure. Whatever you say." I gave him a shove toward Mac and Poppy. "Let's go. They're waiting on us."

Wesley and I were the only people standing up with the bride and groom. I'd asked Poppy why she chose me instead of one of her other friends. "You," she'd told me, "Were the only person not on my payroll who was there for me after my surgery. You're the one I want." I hadn't been able to argue with that.

The ceremony was lovely and blessedly brief. Mac and Poppy's kiss, however, went on long enough to get awkward. When they finally came up for air, I'd expected to follow them down the aisle between the rows of seats. Instead, they stayed where they were. I shot a glance at Wesley, but he just winked at me.

Mac addressed the attendees. "Family and friends, thank you so much for coming. Traditionally the speeches are saved for the reception, but Poppy and I wouldn't be here today if Dad and Keson hadn't introduced us. That's just one of the many reasons they're up here with us right now. After we asked to have the wedding here, my dad made a special request."

What the hell? Mac and Poppy stepped forward, and I started to follow but Tobias put a hand on my shoulder. The newly-weds positioned themselves in the aisle between the first row of seats. What the hell were they going to do?

I was about to look over at Wesley again when everyone in the audience inhaled at once. I jerked my head up, searching for the threat.

"Keson!" Poppy hissed. When I looked at her, she tilted her head toward Wesley.

Wesley, who was down on one knee with a pair of rings on his palm and a loving smile on his face.

Video evidence suggests I gasped and covered my mouth like the winning contestant on *The Bachelor*. I preferred to focus on what happened next.

"Keson," Wesley began in his low, sexy voice. His eyes twin-kled and one side of his mouth quirked up as if he couldn't quite convince himself to be completely serious. "Meeting you, getting to know you, and living with you has been more rewarding than a thousand albums and stadium tours." I held my breath when he paused. "You've filled my life with love and happiness like I've never known. Will you marry me?"

"Yes! Oh, my god, yes!" I shouted. Then I joined him on the ground and, ignoring the rings, I kissed his beautiful mouth.

People cheered and Wesley and I were both leaking tears when I finally pulled back enough to look at the rings. My heart melted. He'd gotten us silicone rings so we wouldn't have to remove them for our respective work.

"I love these," I murmured and kissed him again. "Let's put them on."

Wesley closed his hand around the rings. "Um, Freddy and Poppy said they wouldn't mind, and since Tobias is already here, I thought maybe," he lifted one shoulder and gave me puppy-dog eyes. "Maybe we could get married right now?"

Cheers rang out again from the crowd. I hated to be the voice of reason, but... "Don't we need, like, a license first?"

Wesley waved his hand. "Administrative details. This is about celebrating with our loved ones."

Poppy and Mac were nodding enthusiastically at me. Poppy mouthed "Do it!" and I heard my mother echo her.

It wasn't like I was going to say no, but Wesley could be a steamroller when he got an idea in his head. I liked to give him a little reality check here and there. "I have a condition," I told him.

"Anything." The love shone from his eyes.

I pulled him into a hug and put my mouth to his ear. "I love you, but I'm not changing my last name to Gaylord."

Wesley laughed and hugged me back. "I thought we could both change our names to Lord."

I sealed our bargain with a kiss. "I'm in. Let's do this."

———

True Colors played as Wesley and I slow-danced next to Mac and Poppy. Those two were curled into each other with their heads together, but Wesley would've gotten a crick in his neck if he'd tried to do that while we were vertical. We'd settled for his arms on my shoulders and my arms around his waist.

"You surprised the hell out of me, you know," I remarked.

"I hope it wasn't in a bad way; I didn't want to pressure you."

I squeezed him tight. "No, not at all. I'm excited to be sort-of married to you." He snorted and spun us around. "I meant that the whole commitment thing surprised me. You said in the beginning you were ready to settle down, but I was going to give you another six months before even bringing up marriage because I didn't want you to freak out."

Wesley stopped dancing. He ignored the people staring and cupped my jaw. "Keson, you're my forever person. I'm not afraid of commitment if it's with you."

"Oh," I choked out, blinking back tears. "I love you too." I gathered my precious almost-husband to my chest, and we slowly began moving to the music once more.

———

Thank you for reading *I Touch Hoses*! Curious about how Cole, Will, and Jason got together? Read their story in *Holding On to a Hero*!

ABOUT BIX BARROW

When Bix Barrow got an idea for her first book, it ended up turning into her second — and thus the first two stories in the *Bent Oak, Texas* series emerged. An aspiring author for most of her life, it took a foray into the MM romance genre to spark the steamy scenes and blazing banter Bix now weaves into her novels. Accompanying her on her writing exploits are her two dogs and multitude of cats (six at last count). An avid traveler, Bix has started to view her expeditions as interviews for her future home. Born and raised in Texas, she is eager to move somewhere with fewer politicians, hurricanes, and flooding.

Join Bix Barrow's Boom Boom Room on Facebook for sneak peeks and fun conversation!

Sign up for Bix's newsletter and get a free novella! www.bixbarrow.com

f facebook.com/bixbarrowauthor
instagram.com/bixbarrow
BB bookbub.com/authors/bix-barrow

ALSO BY BIX BARROW

BENT OAK, TEXAS

Holding On to a Hero (Will, Cole, and Jason's story)

Heart Me Up (Craig and Foster's story)

Head Over Feels (Felix and Malcolm's story)

What's Santa Got to Do with It (Steve and Baz's story)

We Don't Need Another Santa (Phillip and Lucas' story)

I Touch Hoses (Keson and Wesley's story) – Related novella

Last Mango in Palm Springs (Ford and Zachary's story) - Related novella

Voices Harry (Mitchell and Harry's story) – Free when you go to www.bixbarrow.com and sign up for my newsletter!

WONDERFALL

Seer (Cal and Greg's story)

Medium (Shane, Ellis, and Rory's story)

Wonder (Simon's story)

LOVE IN MAPLEWOOD (MULTI-AUTHOR SHARED WORLD)

Can You Feel the Maple Tonight (Drake and Finn's story)